WE LOVE TO SURF

By Jeremy Lansing
Illustrated by Michael Lane

www.welovetosurf.us

Printed in the United States of America

ISBN 978-0-9000000-0-0

First Edition

14 13 12 11 10 / 10 9 8 7 6 5 4 3 2 1

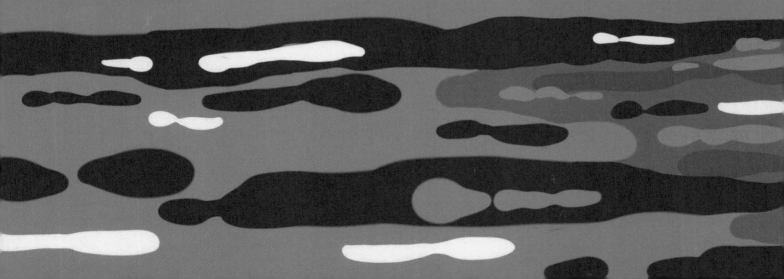

WE LOVE
TO SURF

Dolphins love to surf

Sea turtles love to surf

Birds love to Surf

Sea otters love to surf

Dogs love to surf

Mamas love to surf

Papas love to surf

Kids love to Surf

We love to

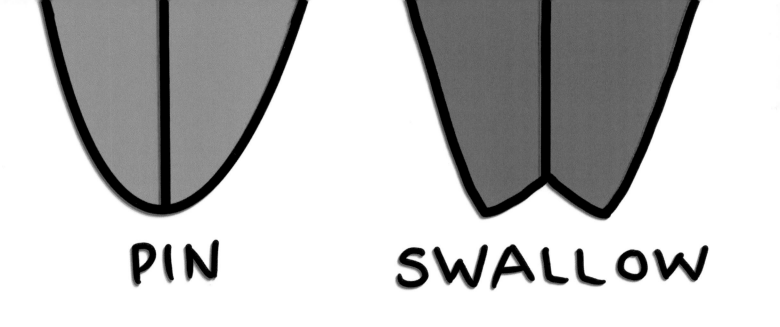

PIN

SWALLOW

DING

FIN BOX

TAIL

SQUASH

FINS

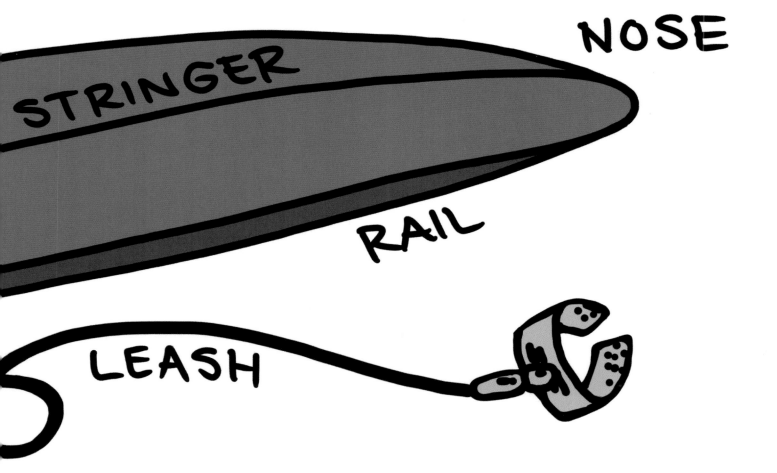

NOSE

STRINGER

RAIL

LEASH

SURF ETIQUETTE

1. FIRST SURFER UP, CLOSEST TO THE CURL HAS RIGHT OF WAY.

2. PADDLE AROUND BREAK TO GET OUT.

3. HANG ON TO YOUR BOARD AND LOOK OUT FOR OTHER SURFERS.

4. HELP OTHER SURFERS IN TROUBLE.

5. RESPECT THE BEACH AND OCEAN.

CPSIA information can be obtained
at www.ICGtesting.com
Printed in the USA
LVIC061119061020
668037LV00001BA/15